For Hazel —E.J.  For Mom —S.G.

A Note About This Story

Water in the Park is an homage to two classic picture books: Alvin Tresselt's 1947 Caldecott Medal–winning *White Snow, Bright Snow,* illustrated by Roger Duvoisin, and Charlotte Zolotow's 1944 *The Park Book,* illustrated by H. A. Rey.

The story comes from my spending early mornings and evenings in Prospect Park, in Brooklyn, New York, one summer when we had many, many ninety-eight-degree days. I watched the people and thought about the way the park's water is used differently by all the inhabitants of the neighborhood, human and animal. —E.J.

Text copyright © 2013 by Emily Jenkins • Jacket art and interior illustrations copyright © 2013 by Stephanie Graegin

All rights reserved. Published in the United States by Schwartz & Wade Books, an imprint of Random House Children's Books, a division of Random House, Inc., New York.

Schwartz & Wade Books and the colophon are trademarks of Random House, Inc.

Visit us on the Web! randomhouse.com/kids

Educators and librarians, for a variety of teaching tools, visit us at RHTeachersLibrarians.com

Library of Congress Cataloging-in-Publication Data
Jenkins, Emily. Water in the park : a book about water and the times of the day / Emily Jenkins. — 1st ed. p. cm.
Summary: Relates how the water in a park is used in different ways by the human and animal inhabitants of a neighborhood.
ISBN 978-0-375-87002-6 (trade) — ISBN 978-0-375-97002-3 (lib. bdg.) [1. Water—Fiction. 2. Parks—Fiction.] I. Title.
PZ7.J4134Wat 2013 [Fic]—dc23 2011050243

The text of this book is set in Hoefler. The illustrations were rendered in pencil-and-ink washes and then assembled and colored digitally. Book design by Rachael Cole

MANUFACTURED IN CHINA • 10 9 8 7 6 5 4 3 2 1 • First Edition

Water in the Park

a book about water & the times of the day

written by **Emily Jenkins**  illustrated by **Stephanie Graegin**

schwartz & wade books · new york

On very hot days,
as the sun rises,
an orange glow shines in the water of the pond.
Just before six o'clock, turtles settle on rocks.
They warm their turtle shells in the light.
Good morning, park!

Most people haven't opened their eyes yet.

Dogs are up, though. Rouw! Rouw! Rouw!

Time for a morning swim.

Today, as soon as Bingo (the first dog)
and his human (the first human)
reach the pond, the turtles slip off their rocks.
More dogs arrive, already panting in the heat.
Heh. Heh. Heh.

Little Nonny has only three legs.

She is learning to swim again after her accident.

Her human scratches her ears.

"Just try it, girl," he says. "You are the dog of all dogs."

Mr. Fluffynut is scared to go deeper than his doggy ankles.

He holds a tennis ball tight in his mouth and will not give it up.

"Drop it!" says his human.

But Mr. Fluffynut will not drop it.

By seven o'clock, two babies have come to the park.

One has a bagel in a brown paper bag.

The other has a plastic box of apple pieces.

The babies want drinks from the water fountain.

They point their baby fingers and jump.

Their grown-ups lift them. Up and up.

At eight, the park attendant turns on the sprinklers.

Whoosh!

Both babies wet their hands in the spray.

One laughs.

The other cries.

On very hot days, puddles ooze across the asphalt by nine o'clock.

Three sparrows hop in

and have their sparrow baths.

The baby with the bagel gives them a snack.

The metal slides are too hot to touch,
but the playground is crowded by ten o'clock.
"Sweating even in the shade," complains Claudie K.'s sitter,
fanning herself with a magazine.
Children pour water down the slides.
Others wait to fill balloons at the fountain.
Shawnee B. dumps pail after pail of water
into the sandbox.

At eleven, volunteers arrive in matching green T-shirts.
They stretch out hoses and water the flower beds.
They pull weeds and snip dead blooms.

Ribbons of water seep out of the rose beds and under benches.
Ants crawl to safety.
Pigeons strut at the edges of the new puddles,
cooling their pigeon ankles.

Coming up on noon, it's time for lunch. Maybe a nap.

Some children cry.

Claudie K. clings to the leg of a bench.
"Not going home," she says. She likes it here.

Around one o'clock, grown-ups wander in, squinting,
from their shops and office buildings.
They sit near the pond and eat sandwiches and yogurt.
Two old people stand with a bag of bread crumbs.
Fish come to the surface.

On very hot days,
the ice cream truck comes early.
By two, its tune is already jingling.
Children coming back to the park
get soft-serve cones and bright Popsicles.
Grown-ups buy bottles of water.
Sticky fingers and faces are rinsed in the sprinkler.

By three, the playground is crowded again.

Shawnee B. dumps pail after pail of water on her mommy's feet.

Big kids fill squirt bottles at the fountain.

Little guys carry water to the sandbox in pails.

They are building a castle in the wet sand.

It is going to have a moat.

Around four o'clock, Benjamin F. skins his knee.

His sitter washes it clean with water from the fountain.

It is so cold! The scrape is bleeding!

He sits on her lap until he feels better.

At five, grown-ups begin squeezing water out of T-shirts.

They find their empty bottles

and pick up bits of broken water balloon.

Some of the children go home in wet clothes.

Others change into dry.

One naughty baby goes home naked.

Claudie K. clings to the chain on her swing.

"Not going home," she says. She likes it here.

The park attendant turns the sprinkler off at six.

One baby laughs when the water disappears.

Another cries.

Then they both go home, drinking water from sippy cups
and clutching their mothers' hands.

It is seven o'clock.

A stripey cat creeps from beneath a bush and laps a quiet puddle.

Tup tup. Tup tup.

And now the dogs come. Rouw! Rouw! Rouw!

Time for an evening swim.

As soon as Bingo (the first dog)

and his human (the first human)

reach the pond, the turtles slide off their rocks.

More dogs race to the water.

Heh. Heh. Heh.

A dad and his boy walk past, on their way home from the diner.

The boy rolls up his pant legs and wades in up to his human ankles.

It's so warm! The rocks are slippery!

Little Nonny stays on the shore this evening.
She is tired.

But Mr. Fluffynut? He finds his own spot by the reeds
and goes all the way in.

His human throws a tennis ball.
Fetch and drop. Fetch and drop.

At eight o'clock, clouds roll in.

The water shines dark, dark blue.

The dogs prick their ears and sniff the air.

The storm comes fast, at the end of this very hot day.

One heavy drop hits the pond—plop!—

and the sky opens.

Water pours down upon the park.

It is almost night, and everyone,

everything,

every*where* in this whole big park,

the benches, the slides, the sandbox,

the rocks, the turtles, the sparrows and pigeons,

the boy and his dad,

Bingo, Mr. Fluffynut, Little Nonny,

the park attendant and one baby up past her bedtime,

animals and humans,

everyone

is now

very, very,

very

wet.

Good night, park.

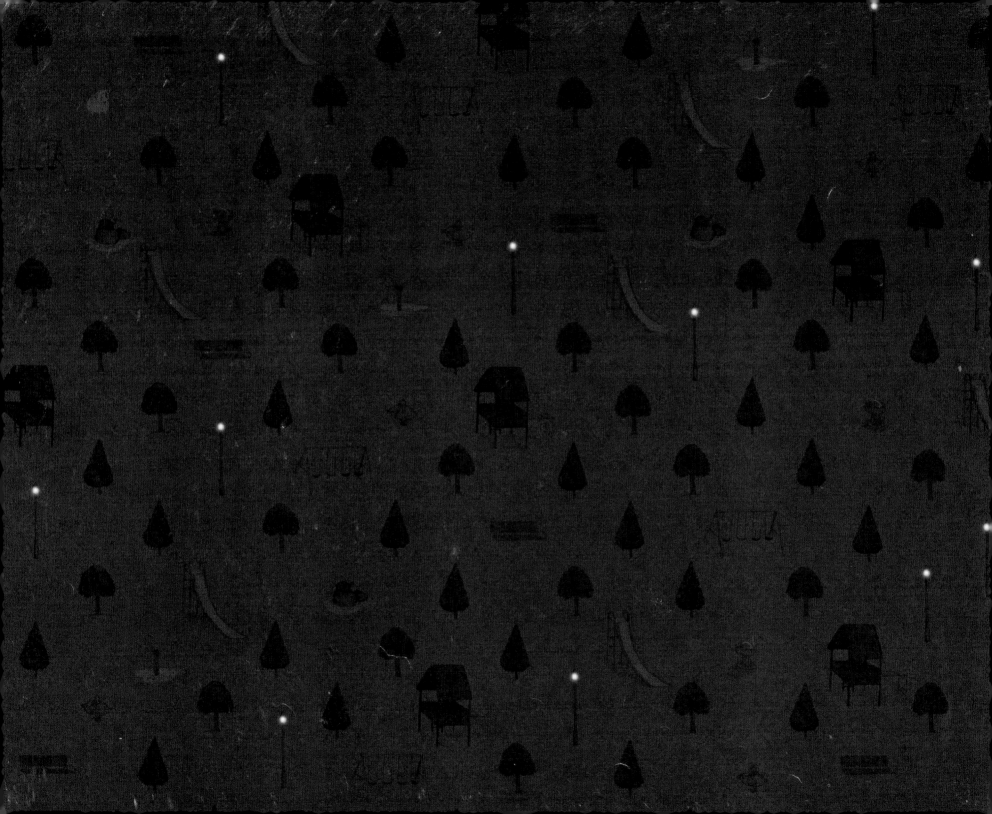